BEAR IN SUN

Written by Stella Blackstone
Illustrated by Debbie Harter

Barefoot Books
better books for children

Bear likes to play
when the sun shines,

Bear likes to sing in the rain.

He flies his red kite
when the wind blows,

**When it's icy,
he skates in the lane.**

Bear likes to paint
when it's misty,

**When storms come,
he hides in his bed.**

When snow falls,
he likes to make snow-bears,

Whatever the weather,
come snow, rain or sun,

Bear always knows
how to have lots of fun!

Spring

Summer

Autumn

Winter

For Felix — S.B.
For Julia and Isabella — D.H.

Barefoot Books
PO Box 95
Kingswood
Bristol BS30 5BH

This book was typeset in Futura
The illustrations were prepared in watercolour, pen and ink and crayon on thick watercolour paper

Graphic design by Polka. Creation, Bath
Colour separation by Grafiscan, Verona
Printed and bound in Singapore by Tien Wah Press Pte Ltd

This book has been printed on 100% acid-free paper

Hardcover ISBN 1 84148 320 6
Paperback ISBN 1 84148 322 2

British Cataloguing-in-Publication Data: a catalogue record for this book
is available from the British Library

1 3 5 7 9 8 6 4 2